Toodles and Teeny

A Story About Friendship

To Wilhelm, dearest husband, living with you
half a century is just the beginning—MBW

To Helene Burgess, a true friend—JN

To my two little turkeys. XO—JA

Published by
MAGINATION PRESS
An Educational Publishing Foundation Book
American Psychological Association
750 First Street, NE
Washington, DC 20002

For more information about our books, including a complete catalog,
please write to us, call 1-800-374-2721, or visit our website at
www.apa.org/pubs/magination.

Printed by Worzalla, Stevens Point, Wisconsin
Book design by Sandra Kimbell

Library of Congress Cataloging-in-Publication Data
Neimark, Jill.
Toodles and Teeny : a story about friendship / Jill Neimark and
Marcella Bakur Weiner ; illustrated by JoAnn Adinolfi.
p. cm.
"American Psychological Association."
Summary: When Toodles the turkey finds a best friend, she excludes
her other barnyard friends until discovering that friendship works best
when it is shared.
ISBN 978-1-4338-1198-2 (hardcover : alk. paper) — ISBN 978-1-
4338-1199-9 (pbk. : alk. paper) [1. Friendship—Fiction. 2. Best
friends—Fiction. 3. Turkeys—Fiction. 4. Domestic animals—Fiction.] I.
Weiner, Marcella Bakur, date. II. Adinolfi, JoAnn, ill. III. Title.
PZ7.N429455To 2012
[E]—dc23
2012019116

Manufactured in the United States of America
First printing August 2012

10 9 8 7 6 5 4 3 2 1

Whoa!

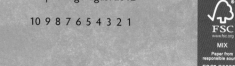

Toodles and Teeny

A Story About Friendship

by Jill Neimark and Marcella Bakur Weiner, EdD, PhD

illustrated by JoAnn Adinolfi

Magination Press • Washington, DC
American Psychological Association

Toodles the Turkey had no best friend.
She had oodles of playmates
And all kinds of play dates

With Cathy the Cow, and Omar the Owl,
With Streaky the Barn Cat
And Boo-Boo the Barn Bat.

All thought Toodles was great, simply first-rate,
But that didn't help.
She felt lonely without a best friend.

And then came a morning when everything changed.
Toodles was down by the pond
Pecking at berries,

When she heard a strange squeak
From a strange bird's strange beak.
"Those berries look yummy!" came a squawk and a squeak.

"Who are you?" said Toodles.

"They call me Teeny," the bird said. "Because I'm so tiny. I'm a turkey like you. And I'm lonely, too."

"Who said I was lonely?
I have oodles of friends."

They stared at each other.

"You're not a turkey," said Toodles.

"I am, I am too! I'm a turkey like you."

Toodles frowned.

Teeny stood there and nodded.

"Would you like to meet tomorrow?"
said Teeny. "I'll bring you some
chestnuts I saved for my birthday."

"I do enjoy chestnuts," Toodles admitted.
"Okay. I'll see you tomorrow."

"Bye, Toodles," said Teeny.
Toodles waved and ran off.

That night Toodles fell fast asleep
With a smile in her heart.

Somehow she knew
She had found a best friend.

That whole summer long, Toodles and Teeny

Met by the pond, ate berries and chestnuts,

Took long naps
on the hillside,

told silly stories,

Talked about nothing
and talked about everything.

Back at the farm the animals wondered
Where Toodles was going all day.
Why didn't she play with them anymore?

They all marched down to the pond.
Toodles and Teeny lay on their backs,
Feet up in the air, taking a nap.

The animals pointed and laughed. Toodles woke up.

"Go ahead, Toodles, play with your
new friend. We truly don't miss you.
We don't even care!"

Toodles couldn't believe it.

"I'm sorry, Toodles," said Teeny.
"You'd better go home now."

"I can't leave you, Teeny.
You're my best friend!
And you know what that means.

"A best friend cries with you when you feel hurt.
A best friend hugs you when you feel sad.
A best friend holds your hand when you need to be brave.
A best friend tells everyone how special you are.
A best friend is there when you are in need."

"We're best friends!" said Teeny.
"But don't you miss all your other friends, too?"

"I do, yes, I do," said Toodles.

"Maybe we should go talk to your friends," said Teeny.

Toodles looked scared.
"What if they laugh at us again?"

"You'll know just what to say," Teeny said.
"You're their good friend.
And I believe in you."

So Toodles and Teeny walked back to the farm.
Nobody turned. Nobody looked.

"Hi, everybody," said Toodles, "It's me."

"I want to introduce you to my new friend, Teeny.
                    She's funny and sweet,
                    and she's really quite nice."

"Why should we care?" shouted Streaky the Barn Cat. "You ignored us all summer. You left us behind!"

"I'm sorry," said Toodles. "I didn't mean to. I just never had a best friend before."

And then Teeny stepped up.
"I know it's not right, and you feel left out. But for sure
Toodles loves you. She told me so many stories about
each one of you.
Like Streaky, the day you jumped in the paint can
And came out covered with red from head to tail!
Then you rolled in the grass every which way. You painted
the green grass red!"

We remember that! That was so funny!
What else did Toodles tell you about us?"

And they gathered around to listen and laugh.
They forgot their hurt feelings. They knew Toodles
loved them. They were still her good friends.

Soon it was night and Teeny had to go home.
"Come back tomorrow!" said Cathy the Cow.
"Our home is your home!" said Boo-Boo the Barn Bat.
"Good friends forever!" said Goopy the Goat.
"Toodles was right," said Streaky the Barn Cat.
"What she said is true. She found a real best friend,
when she found you."

Note to Parents

By Marcella Bakur Weiner, EdD, PhD, and Jill Neimark

Friends are the heart of existence at any age. They expand our range of experience and teach us about our own capacities—for accomplishment, kindness, fairness, compassion, forgiveness, and ultimately, the depth and breadth of the self. Friends are chosen because, in one or many ways, they add to the joy of being alive. Friends are part of who we are, and they often reflect who we wish to become. Above all, friendship teaches trust. To trust others, and to trust oneself, is the bedrock of healthy intimacy. In *Toodles and Teeny,* Toodles shows Teeny she can be trusted to be loyal when she refuses to abandon her. Teeny steps up to defend Toodles to all her friends, unafraid of rejection. And Toodles' friends realize that they still love her, and she loves them—that they are still good friends. Because they trust that friendship, they are even able to acknowledge that Teeny is a worthwhile best friend. "Toodles was right," said Streaky the Barn Cat. "What she said is true. She found a real best friend, when she found you."

The Value of Best Friends and Good Friends
Friends come in many varieties. Your child may have one unique "best" friend—a very special person with whom your child is able to be herself, share secrets, and feel understood. Over time, as the friendship is nurtured, best friends come to instinctively know each other, and deeply feel what the other feels. As Toodles says to her best friend Teeny, "A best friend cries with you when you feel hurt. A best friend hugs you when you feel sad. A best friend holds your hand when you need to be brave. A best friend tells everyone how special you are." Because of that deep connection, the first best friend of childhood is a monumental experience.

However, good friends are just as important in childhood as best friends. Though your child may not share his deepest secrets with his good friends, he may enjoy their company, laugh with them, or share similar interests. Not everybody can be a best friend. A child's self-esteem and sense of belonging are very dependent on peer acceptance by a network of good friends—at school, in the neighborhood, at summer camp, or in extra-curricular activities. Acceptance by a network of good friends is linked to self-esteem, social competence, and even academic achievement. Good friends lessen the risk of bullying by others, and can even buffer children from family troubles.

**How to Help Your Child
Build and Maintain Friendships**
Learning to build friendships is one of the ways children develop into well-rounded, emotionally healthy human beings. You can help your child nurture and maintain friendships in a number of ways.

Help your child realize his own strengths. This helps build self-esteem, one of the foundations for making and being a good friend. Encourage your child to explore and discover his own unique personality and talents. Point out the traits that make your child a good friend. You may say something like, "Your sense of humor makes you so fun to be around," or "You're great at coming up with ideas for fun things to do."

Create opportunities for socializing. If your child is having difficulty making friends, you can call up a neighbor or classmate's parents to organize a play date. One-on-one play dates are a good place to start, as groups of three or larger may leave one member feeling left out. If your child is feeling awkward, it will help to have some structure in place—plan an activity in advance, such as a craft or video game, and limit the play date to a few hours. Before the play date, you can coach your child on how to behave; for example, practice sharing and taking turns. You can also consider signing your child up for a team sport, or another group activity such as a pottery class. Keep in mind that your child may have a different social style than you do—it's okay if he prefers hanging out with friends one-on-one rather than in big groups.

Teach the value of acceptance and forgiveness. Your child may be upset because her friend becomes busy or distracted for a while, and does not call as often. Perhaps a friend unintentionally hurt your child's feelings. Or perhaps her friend is struggling with her own problems and is not as giving as she once was. Let your child know that this is all just part of life and a good friend learns to stay steadfast through the ups and downs, the good times and bad, and to accept and forgive. Good friends know they can trust each other to care and support each other, and that whatever flaws they each have, they will forgive each other anyway.

Emphasize being a good friend. In order to maintain good friendships, children need to learn to *be* a good friend. Learning how to be a good friend means developing good listening skills, showing empathy, resolving conflicts effectively, and most of all, understanding the perspective of others. If your child hurts a friend's feelings, encourage him to mend the rift with a heartfelt apology, such as, "I am really, really sorry. I feel really, really bad that I hurt your feelings—I didn't mean it. I hope you will forgive me."

Coach your child through friendship ups and downs. As children begin to explore good friends and best friends, they will experience ups and downs. Their friendships may go through phases. If at one time a good friend seems to have temporarily lost interest because of new activities or friendships, you can coach your child to say something like, "Ellen, you always call for me to go to school together in the morning. You haven't done that in the last few days and I miss you. Do you still feel the same about our friendship,

or is something bothering you? I want it to be like it was. Please tell me how you're feeling."

If a new best friend threatens your child's other friendships, you can teach your child to say something like this: "Lucy, you and I have been friends for a long time. Now that Susie is here and I also play with her, it does not mean I don't really, really like you. I do. She can never give me what I got from you, and still do. You and she are two different people, but know that you have not lost me as a friend. No way. I am your friend, like always."

Help your child cope with rejection. As children get older, they become more selective with their friendships—as a result, your child may feel rejected or excluded by her friends at some point. You can help by listening and offering a sympathetic ear. Focus on coming up with ways to cope, and ask your child constructive questions, such as "Is there anything else you can try?" or "What can you do to feel better?" Try to help your child figure out the solution on her own. If you suspect your child is being systematically excluded or bullied, it may be helpful to talk to a professional.

Know when to step back. It can be hard to see your child struggling to navigate peer relationships; however, learning to deal with peer relations on their own is one way that children grow and gain strength and resilience. You will always be there as a source of love and support for your child. Eventually, however, she will have to interact with peers and deal with difficult peer relationships on her own. As the parent, you can help by practicing with your child what she is going to say to a classmate or friend, doing a role-play, discussing the best ways to handle a difficult situation, and talking to her about a tough day and sharing your experiences.

You are, in all likelihood, the best resource for guiding your child through the ups and downs of friendship. However, if your child's distress persists or interferes with daily activities, it may be time to consult a licensed psychologist or psychotherapist for further guidance.

About the Authors

Jill Neimark is an author of fiction and nonfiction, an award-winning science journalist, and a contributing editor to *Discover* magazine. Her credits include the middle-grade novel *The Secret Spiral*, the adult novel *Bloodsong*, which was a Book of the Month Club selection and published in five countries, and the adult nonfiction title *Why Good Things Happen to Good People: How to Live a Longer, Healthier, Happier Life by the Simple Act of Giving* (coauthored with bioethicist Stephen Post, PhD). It was awarded the Kama Prize in Medical Humanities by World Literacy Canada in 2008. A sequel to *The Secret Spiral*, entitled *The Golden Rectangle*, is out in February of 2013.

Marcella Bakur Weiner, EdD, PhD, is a fellow of the American Psychological Association and adjunct professor at Marymount Manhattan College in New York City. She is also president of the Mapleton-Midwood Community Mental Health Center and was chief staff psychologist at the Park Slope Children's Center in Brooklyn, New York. Dr. Weiner has authored twenty-five books and seventy-five journal articles, and she has been interviewed for numerous national television shows, radio talk shows, and magazine articles. Her most recent book is *Women Psychotherapists: Journeys in Healing*, coauthored with Lillian Comas-Diaz.

About the Illustrator

JoAnn Adinolfi was born in New York City, on Staten Island. She is the author and illustrator of *Tina's Diner* and is the illustrator of *Halloween Hoots and Howls* and *The Perfect Thanksgiving,* among dozens of other children's books. She lives in Portsmouth, New Hampshire.

Together Neimark and Weiner authored and Adinolfi illustrated the Magination Press book, *I Want Your Moo,* a 2010 Learning Magazine® Teachers' Choice Award℠ for Children's Books.

About Magination Press

Magination Press is an imprint of the American Psychological Association, the largest scientific and professional organization representing psychologists in the United States and the largest association of psychologists worldwide.